To Jake, who forges his own path with light,
laughter, and love . . . and is most
definitely wonderful!
—D.G.

To Cristina and Giovanna, my best friends at
school. Being with them was always wonderful!
—F.C.

Text copyright © 2021 by Donna Gephart
Illustrations copyright © 2021 Francesca Chessa
All Rights Reserved
HOLIDAY HOUSE is registered in the U.S. Patent and Trademark Office.
Printed and bound in November 2020 at Toppan Leefung, DongGuan, China.
The artwork was created with colored pencils, watercolors, and digital tools.
www.holidayhouse.com
First Edition
1 3 5 7 9 10 8 6 4 2

Library of Congress Cataloging-in-Publication Data

Names: Gephart, Donna, author. | Chessa, Francesca, illustrator.
Title: Go be wonderful! / by Donna Gephart ; illustrated by Francesca Chessa.
Description: First edition. | New York : Holiday House, [2021] | Audience:
Ages 4–8. | Audience: Grades K–1. | Summary: "When Daisy is born, her
parents tell her to 'go be wonderful,' and by being herself, she is!
Each year presents new milestones with humor and love" —Provided by publisher.
Identifiers: LCCN 2020007646 | ISBN 9780823445110 (hardcover)
Subjects: CYAC: Self-confidence—Fiction. | Growth—Fiction. | Family
Life—Fiction.
Classification: LCC PZ7.G293463 Go 2021 | DDC [E]—dc23
LC record available at https://lccn.loc.gov/2020007646

ISBN: 978-0-8234-4511-0 (hardcover)

Go Be Wonderful!

Donna Gephart

illustrated by Francesca Chessa

HOLIDAY HOUSE · NEW YORK

WHEN Daisy was born, Daddy held her close and whispered, "Go be wonderful."

And she was.

She CRIED and ate.

She CRIED and slept.

And she went poo.

She giggled through 1,258,364 games of Peekaboo.

When Daisy turned one, Mommy twirled her and whirled her and sang, "Go be wonderful."

And she was.

She zoomed her truck.

She dressed the dog. Poor Mr. Bonkers!

And she joined a rock-and-roll band.

Daisy was the star.

When Daisy turned two,
Grandma and Grandpa covered
her with smooches and said,
"Go be wonderful."

And she was.

She shopped for food.

She fed the dog.

At bedtime she stamped her foot, crossed her arms, and yelled, "NOOOOOOOOOOOOOOO!"

But she went to bed anyway,
after six sips of water, seven
sleepy stories, and one burpy,
slurpy kiss from Mr. Bonkers.

When Daisy turned three, Uncle Jay,
Uncle Denny, and Uncle Michael danced a
jiggly jig and crooned, "Go be wonderful."

And she was.

She used the potty.

"Wheee!"
She took a bath.

After her second splashy bath,
Daisy spun round and round . . .

until she was dry
and dizzy and—
PLOP!—toppled over.

Then she wiggled and tugged her clothes on ALL BY HERSELF.

When Daisy turned four, her neighbor Ms. Myrna
tweaked her cheeks and twittered, "Go be wonderful."

And she was.

She raked the leaves.

She hopped on one foot.

And she rode her scooter
all the way to the library...
where she chose a book all by herself.

It was time for Daisy to start school. Daddy, Mommy, Grandma and Grandpa, Uncle Jay, Uncle Denny, Uncle Michael, and her neighbor Ms. Myrna fussed over her.

They all said, "Go be wonderful!"

But Daisy wasn't sure she'd be wonderful at school.

What if she put her brand-new lunch box in the wrong place?

What if she put it in the right place, but no one liked her?

What if she got lost on her way to the bathroom?

What if she cried because she missed Mr. Bonkers?

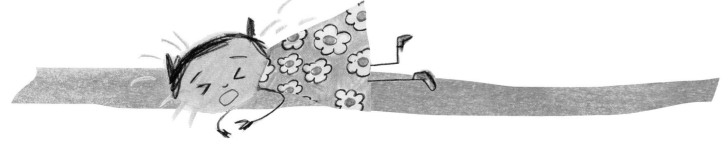

What if . . . ?

Daisy worried about all the things that *might* happen at school.

Here's what *did* happen. . . .

Daisy played Peekaboo with Fluffy and Slimy, the class pets.

Then she put her lunch box in the almost-right place.

She zoomed like a truck at recess.

And bumped into only two people . . . by accident.

At snack time, Daisy shared her bench.

And spilled juice on her new top.

But so did Zeta.

And she found the potty . . . just in time.

"Whew!"

Then Daisy listened as Ms. Marlow read a story
about a dog, who was just like Mr. Bonkers . . .
and it was wonderful.

When Daisy burst from her classroom at the end of the school day, she said, "Guess what?"

"I was wonderful!"